TITCHY WITCH and the Birthday Broomstick

For Kaia
R.I.

To Nick
K.M.

Orchard Books
96 Leonard Street, London EC2A 4XD
Orchard Books Australia
32/45-51 Huntley Street, Alexandria, NSW 2015
First published in Great Britain in 2003
First paperback publication 2004
ISBN 1 84121 044 7 (HB)
ISBN 1 84121 120 6 (PB)
Text © Rose Impey 2003 Illustrations © Katharine McEwen 2003
A CIP catalogue record for this book is available from the British Library
1 3 5 7 9 10 8 6 4 2 (HB)
3 5 7 9 10 8 6 4 (PB)
Printed in Hong Kong

TITCHY WITCH and the Birthday Broomstick

Rose Impey ★ Katharine McEwen

ORCHARD BOOKS

Titchy-witch

Victor

Eric

Wendel

Weeny-witch

Witchy-witch

Cat-a-bogus

Titchy-witch woke up, itchy-scratchy with excitement.
Today she was seven witch-years old.

She peeped in on Mum and
Dad, but they were still asleep.

Weeny-witch was still asleep too.

Cat-a-bogus opened one eye, then closed it again.

Even Eric was still dozing.

So Titchy-witch
went to watch
for the post. Mr P
flew in with four
parcels.

Titchy-witch grabbed the biggest
parcel and opened it.
Her first broomstick!
Titchy-witch jumped on and
held tight.

But nothing happened.
Mr P squawked with
laughter. Titchy-witch gave
him a little witchy stare.

She didn't know much magic yet,
but she was sure she could turn
him into a turnip, if she tried.

Now Mum and Dad were up,
Titchy-witch wanted to learn
to fly, this minute.

But Witchy-witch and Wendel were off to work.

"Cat-a-bogus will show you," they called. And they disappeared in a swirl of dust.

Cat-a-bogus had better things to do,
but he did like showing off.

"We'll start with a few rules,"
he hissed.

"Number one: no flying outside."
"Yes, yes," said Titchy-witch.

"Number two: hold on with both hands."
"Yes, yes, yes," said Titchy-witch.

"Number three: no standing up!"
Standing up! Titchy-witch hadn't even thought of that!

At last Cat-a-bogus told her the
magic words.

"Zig-a-zag-a-zoom,
fly this broomstick
round the room!"

But, even with the magic
words, flying wasn't easy.
Titchy-witch kept sliding off.

Or bumping into things.

Bang! Smash! She crashed
into the ceiling.

"Dive!" growled Cat-a-bogus.

18

So Titchy-witch dived.
And, suddenly, she was flying.

"I can fly!" she squealed.
"Watch me! Watch me!"

But the cat had better things
to do than watch a little witch.
He left Titchy-witch giving
Victor a ride.

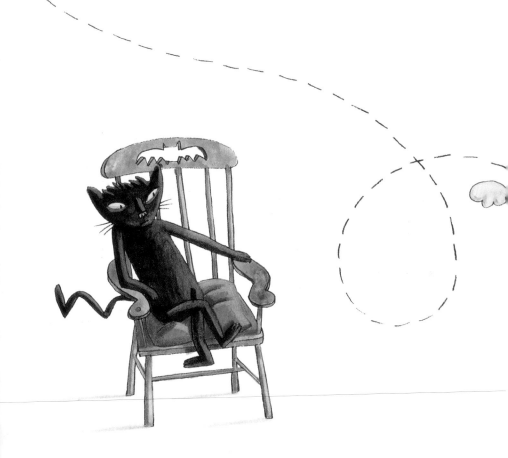

All day, they flew round the house, until Victor felt quite dizzy. "Flying's easy-breezy," said Titchy-witch.

She thought it was *so* easy,
she started to break the rules.

Then Titchy-witch broke the most important rule. She opened the window and flew outside!

"Zig-a-zag-a-zoom, fly this broomstick out of this room!"

Oh, dear!

The broomstick zoomed over
the roof of the house.
It flew so fast it almost hit
the chimney.

Now Titchy-witch felt dizzy too.
She wanted to stop, but she
didn't know how to.

It was getting dark. Suddenly,
something came flying towards
her. It was Witchy-witch,
hurrying home.

She had to swerve to miss
Titchy-witch. And *something* fell
off the back of her broomstick.

Down...

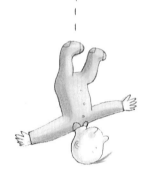

down...

down...it fell.

But Titchy-witch knew what to do.
She dived down, just in time to
catch Weeny-witch.

The baby squealed with delight. She liked flying too.

Because it was her birthday,
Mum and Dad weren't too
cross with Titchy-witch.
They had a special birthday tea.

Maggots and mash!
And beetle juice jelly for afters!

That night, Titchy-witch went to sleep hugging her broomstick, and dreaming about flying.

TITCHY WITCH

Rose Impey ★ Katharine McEwen

Enjoy a little more magic with all the Titchy-witch tales:

❏ Titchy-witch and the Birthday Broomstick   1 84121 120 6

❏ Titchy-witch and the Disappearing Baby   1 84121 116 8

❏ Titchy-witch and the Frog Fiasco   1 84121 122 2

❏ Titchy-witch and the Stray Dragon   1 84121 118 4

❏ Titchy-witch and the Bully-Boggarts   1 84121 124 9

❏ Titchy-witch and the Wobbly Fang   1 84121 126 5

❏ Titchy-witch and the Get-Better Spell   1 84121 128 1

❏ Titchy-witch and the Halloween Party   1 84121 130 3

All priced at £4.99 each

Colour Crunchies are available from all good
bookshops, or can be ordered direct from the publisher:
Orchard Books, PO BOX 29, Douglas IM99 1BQ
Credit card orders please telephone 01624 836000
or fax 01624 837033
or e-mail: bookshop@enterprise.net for details.

To order please quote title, author and ISBN
and your full name and address.
Cheques and postal orders should be
made payable to 'Bookpost plc'.
Postage and packing is FREE within the UK
(overseas customers should add £1.00 per book).

Prices and availability are subject to change.